GLOBETROTTERS

UNITED STATES

Jane Hinchey

REDBACK publishing

First Published 2024 by
Redback Publishing
PO Box 357 Frenchs Forest NSW 2086
Australia

www.redbackpublishing.com
orders@redbackpublishing.com

© Redback Publishing 2024

ISBN 978-1-761400-51-3

Author: Jane Hinchey
Editor: Caroline Thomas
Design: Redback Publishing

Original illustrations © Redback Publishing 2024
Originated by Redback Publishing

Acknowledgements
Abbreviations: l—left, r—right, b—bottom, t—top, c—centre, m—middle
We would like to thank the following for permission to reproduce photographs: (Images © shutterstock, wikimediacommons), p4bl Yolshin/Shutterstock.com, p6bl View Apart/Shutterstock.com, p9tl VanderWolf Images/Shutterstock.com, p11tr George Sheldon/Shutterstock.com, p11ml Joseph Sohm/Shutterstock.com, p12tl Gregory Johnston/Shutterstock.com, p12bl Floyd Davidson, CC BY-SA 4.0 <https://creativecommons.org/licenses/by-sa/4.0>, via Wikimedia Commons, p13tl aceshot1/Shutterstock.com, p13mr Carol M. Highsmith, Public domain, via Wikimedia Commons, p13br Sergii Figurnyi/Shutterstock.com, p15tl photo.ua/Shutterstock.com, p17br Sina Ettmer Photography/Shutterstock.com, p16tr Wileydoc/Shutterstock.com, p17tr Steve Jacobson/Shutterstock.com, p19tr Tami Freed/Shutterstock.com, p20tr turtix/Shutterstock.com, p20ml Featureflash Photo Agency/Shutterstock.com, p21ml Sean Pavone/Shutterstock.com, p21bl Roy Harris/Shutterstock.com, p24bl ARM Photo Video/Shutterstock.com, p28tr unknown author, Public domain, via Wikimedia Commons, p28br Harper's, Public domain, via Wikimedia Commons, p29tc Phillip Kraskoff/Shutterstock.com, p29br catwalker/Shutterstock.com

Disclaimer
Every effort has been made to contact copyright holders of any material reproduced in this book. Any omissions will be rectified in subsequent printings if notice is given to the publisher.

A catalogue record for this book is available from the National Library of Australia

CONTENTS

MAP OF THE USA

Alaska

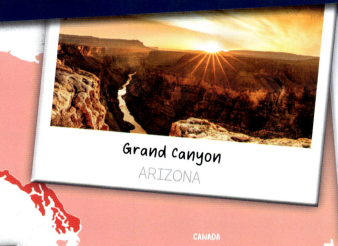
Grand canyon
ARIZONA

Statue of Liberty
NEW YORK CITY

CANADA

Hawaii

Seattle

Mount Rushmore

ROUTE 66

Chicago

New York

Washington

San Francisco

WELCOME LAS VEGAS NEVADA

Las Vegas

Los Angeles

Dallas

Miami

CENTRAL AMERICA

Hawaii

Alaska

Did you know?

The USA – Canada border is 8,890 kilometres long, making it the longest international border in the world.

4

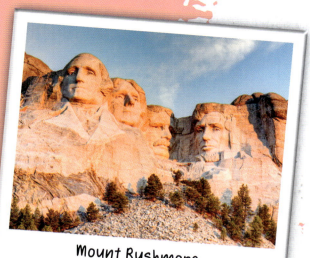
Mount Rushmore
SOUTH DAKOTA

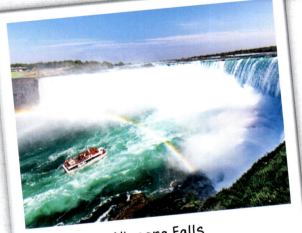
Niagara Falls
NEW YORK STATE

Disneyland
CALIFORNIA

SNAPSHOT

COUNTRY

The United States of America (USA)

CAPITAL

Washington DC

AREA	POPULATION
9,833,517 square kilometres	334,233,854 (2023)

MAIN LANGUAGES

English and Spanish (no official language)

CURRENCY	$ US dollar
GOVERNMENT	Federal democratic republic

WELCOME TO THE USA

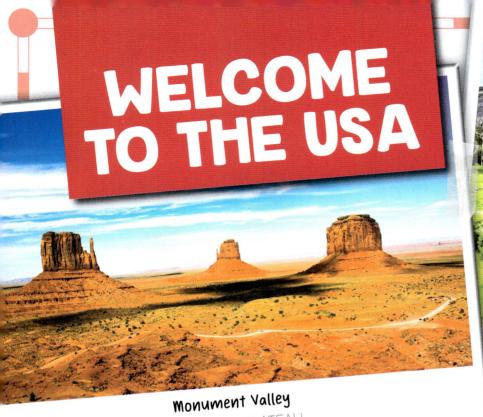

Monument Valley
COLORADO PLATEAU

Yellowstone National Park
WYOMING

The United States of America is the third largest country in the world by population. It is located on the continent of North America and shares land borders with Canada to the north and with Mexico to the south. The Atlantic Ocean forms its eastern border and the Pacific Ocean forms a border to the west. The USA is a geographically diverse country, with stunning mountain ranges, rolling plains and valleys, and pristine lakes and river systems.

New York City
NEW YORK STATE

People have lived in the region for tens of thousands of years. In recent times, the USA has become a strong nation with a diverse, multicultural society built on a large immigrant population.

States and Regions

There are 50 states in the USA, with 49 states on the mainland, and Hawaii located in the Pacific Ocean. There are vast regional differences across the country.

The 50 States of America

WASHINGTON
OREGON
MONTANA
IDAHO
WYOMING
NEVADA
UTAH
CALIFORNIA
COLORADO
ARIZONA
NEW MEXICO

NORTH DAKOTA
MINNESOTA
SOUTH DAKOTA
WISCONSIN
MICHIGAN
NEBRASKA
IOWA
ILLINOIS
INDIANA
OHIO
KANSAS
MISSOURI

VERMONT
MAINE
NEW HAMPSHIRE
MASSACHUSETTS
NEW YORK
RHODE ISLAND
CONNECTICUT
PENNSYLVANIA
NEW JERSEY
DELAWARE
MARYLAND
DC

WEST VIRGINIA
VIRGINIA
KENTUCKY
NORTH CAROLINA
TENNESSEE
SOUTH CAROLINA

OKLAHOMA
ARKANSAS
MISSISSIPPI
ALABAMA
GEORGIA
TEXAS
LOUISIANA
FLORIDA

ALASKA
HAWAII

The USA is divided into six main regions:

- New England
- The Mid-Atlantic
- The South
- The Southwest
- The West
- The Midwest

The Capitol Building in Washington DC is the headquarters of the United States congress

Government

The United States is a democratic country and a constitution-based federal republic. The Federal Government is composed of three branches: legislative, executive and judicial.

Every four years, citizens over the age of 18 can vote to elect the President of the United States. The President can only serve two terms in office.

The White House

The President works and lives in the White House, in Washington DC. The White House was built between 1792 and 1800 and it has 132 rooms, including 32 bathrooms. The first President to live there was John Adams.

The White House
WASHINGTON DC

Main Industries

The most important industries include services, automotive, energy, mining, technology, manufacturing and agriculture.

Morenci Copper Mine
ARIZONA

Natural Resources

The United States (US) has one of the world's largest reserves of coal. Other resources include petroleum, iron ore, potash, timber, nickel, gold, copper, zinc and lead.

Agriculture

The US produces crops such as wheat, barley, oats, rye, corn (maize), sugarcane, potatoes, mixed grains, cotton and hemp, as well as livestock, dairy and poultry, and horticulture.

The United States is a multicultural country, with a population of over 334 million people. Indigenous people lived there long before it was settled by the British. More recently, immigrants from all over Europe, Asia, and Central and South America have arrived.

Latino Americans

There are more than 50 million Hispanic and Latino Americans. This makes them the largest minority group in the United States. The 500-year-long influence of the Latino community can be seen right across the country, in food, music, media and language.

African Americans

Approximately 47 million Americans identify as black. While many black Americans can trace multiple generations of their families, there are a rising number of black immigrants from Africa and the Caribbean. For those who identify as African American, it can be difficult to trace family histories prior to the 1870 census. This is due to slavery and a lack of record-keeping.

Amish People

Members of this conservative Christian Church arrived in Pennsylvania in the early 18th century. They remain the largest Amish community in the country, numbering around 30,000. The Amish continue to live as they did when they first arrived and do not engage with the modern American lifestyle. Amish people do not accept modern conveniences or technologies.

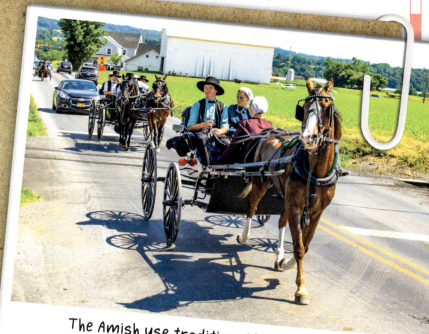

The Amish use traditional horse-drawn carriages for transportation

The Vietnamese-American community celebrates Tet Lunar New Year

Vietnamese Americans

After the Vietnam War (1954–1975), America accepted over 120,000 Vietnamese refugees. Today, there are approximately 2.2 million Americans of Vietnamese descent.

Irish Americans

The Irish began emigrating to America to escape from famine at home. Between 1820 and 1930, approximately 4.5 million Irish people arrived in America. Today, around 10% of the population has Irish heritage.

AMERICAN INDIAN PEOPLE

America's First Nations people have lived in the region for thousands of years. They are also called Native people, Native Americans, or American Indians, but generally they identify according to their tribe. There are 574 federally recognised tribes, whose ways of life vary greatly due to vast geographical differences. Today, some Native Americans still live on reservations and continue their rich cultural and ancestral practices.

Dancers participate at the Julyamsh Powwow in Idaho

American Indian Tribes hold powwows to celebrate and showcase dance, music, food, arts and crafts. The word powwow comes from the Algonquian word pau-wau, which means 'healing ceremony'.

Inupiat family in Alaska

Fast Fact

There are 229 federally and state-recognised tribes in Alaska – the largest number in the United States.

The Gathering of Nations is the largest Indian powwow in North America

Tribal Distinctions

American Indian tribes vary greatly across the country, with vastly different languages and cultural practices. Some of the most well-known tribes are the Cherokee, Apache, Sioux, and Navajo.

Cherokee

The largest tribe is the Cherokee. Before European settlers arrived, they lived in an area of the southeastern United States. They grew corn, beans and squash, and hunted animals for food.

In 1835, some Cherokee were forced to sign a treaty that gave the United States all their land in exchange for some land in Oklahoma and five million dollars. The people from the Cherokee, Chickasaw, Choctaw, Muscogee and Seminole tribes were then marched at gunpoint from North Carolina to Oklahoma. This is now referred to as the Trail of Tears.

Cherokee chiefs and warriors wore a headdress to symbolise bravery and honour

Navajo

The Navajo people lived in the areas now known as Arizona and New Mexico. They fished and hunted, and are known for their traditional arts such as dance, jewellery making and wood carving. In modern times, the Navajo culture has gained popularity through movies and television and this has fuelled efforts to revive and protect their traditional cultural and spiritual practices.

Traditional craft methods are used on the Navajo nation reservation in Arizona

WHERE AMERICANS LIVE

The US is a huge country, with around 40% of the population living in the eastern states. Over 80% of the population lives in towns and cities.

children in remote northern areas cope with extreme weather conditions

Rural Areas

There are sparsely populated wilderness areas across Wyoming, North Dakota, South Dakota and Montana, but Alaska is by far the least densely populated state.

Northern Lights

Fairbanks, Alaska is the coldest city in the USA. It has a population of nearly 33,000 people. From August to April, the aurora borealis, (also known as the northern lights), can be seen. For seventy days of each year, Fairbanks experiences 24 hours of sunlight.

The aurora borealis is a spectacular natural light show caused by solar storms

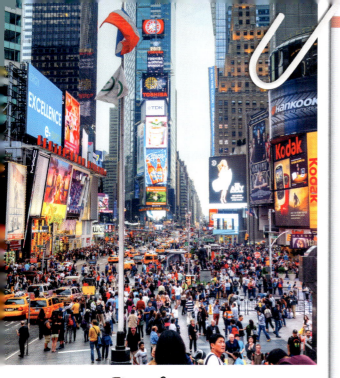

Times Square
NEW YORK CITY

Towns and Cities

The largest city in the US is New York, with nearly 19 million people living in the New York metropolitan area.

Other densely populated areas are Los Angeles, Chicago, Houston and Miami. Residents have access to good infrastructure, shopping, markets and restaurants. People play sports, visit galleries and museums, and attend events. Families generally have access to a range of school and medical facilities. However, while many Americans live a comfortable life, the poverty rate remains a problem, with 11.6% of the population living under the poverty line in 2021.

The Empire State Building

The Empire State Building rises 102 stories above New York City. It is the city's most iconic building and one of the most famous structures in the world. The Empire State was the first building to exceed 100 floors and remains one of New York's and the world's most iconic skyscrapers. It's so famous that it has featured in over 250 films.

The Empire State Building
NEW YORK CITY

Did you know?

The US is so large that it spans six time zones.

DAILY LIFE

The United States is one of the wealthiest countries in the world and the standard of living is generally very high. Americans have access to education and infrastructure, and there is much to do and experience. Americans are well-known for their love of sport, films and music events. They savour their leisure time and cultural pursuits. All over the country, people belong to cultural and sports clubs.

Family is very important. Most households consist of a nuclear family, but many different families from immigrant backgrounds live in multi-generational homes. For all Americans, it is common for extended family to come together to share special occasions with loved ones.

Thanksgiving

One important annual holiday is Thanksgiving, held annually on the fourth Thursday in November. The first Thanksgiving was a meal shared between the pilgrims and the Wampanoag Indians, who were native to the area. Today, most Americans see the day as an opportunity to spend time with loved ones.

Americans love sports, and the country has produced some of the greatest athletes of all time. The three major American sports are football, basketball and baseball. Other popular sports include golf, soccer, ice hockey, tennis and skiing.

A LOVE OF SPORTS

32 NFL teams compete to reach the Super Bowl

The Super Bowl

The biggest event on the sporting calendar each year is the Super Bowl. This is the final play-off game of the National Football League (NFL) to determine the league champion for the year. The game is played on the second Sunday in February.

◯ Lebron James

Basketball

Basketball competitions are run by the NBA (National Basketball Association). The NBA is followed by fans all around the world. Some of the superstars of basketball include LeBron James, Kevin Durant and Michael Jordan.

EDUCATION

In the United States, every child has a right to a free school education, so children can attend city, state, or federal government-funded public schools.

School starts by age six and continues until 16 to 18 years of age. Generally, the standard is high, with children studying subjects such as reading, writing, mathematics, science, social studies and arts. Some schools offer foreign languages, sports programs, and even vocational skills.

Other types of schooling include free charter schools, church schools, and expensive private schools. The school year starts in September and ends in June. Students who attend public schools don't wear school uniforms.

Did You Know?

Low-income students can apply for support for breakfast and lunch for free or a minimal price.

LANGUAGE

The United States does not have an official language, but the most commonly spoken language is English. There are also more than 42 million speakers of Spanish in the United States.

Other commonly spoken languages include Chinese, French, Tagalog, Vietnamese, German and Korean.

Native American Languages

Native American languages consist of dozens of distinct language families as well as many individual languages. There are 167 Native American languages currently spoken, although many of these are at risk. Some of the most widely spoken are Navajo and Western Apache.

Language is an important part of cultural identity and there are now many programs that address the issue of teaching language to young people.

THE ARTS

The United States has produced many great performers, writers, painters and musicians.

Hollywood stars promote their latest films by attending red carpet premieres

Hollywood

While America's film industry began in New York, film companies began locating to Southern California, near Los Angeles, because of the year-round good weather. Today, Hollywood is home to the most successful film industry in the world, and the place of countless dreams. While movies are made all over the world, Hollywood is still the heart of the entertainment business.

No art form is more American than Jazz. It sprang from the African American community in New Orleans in the late 1800s, taking the country by storm. The 1920s are often called the Jazz Age. Jazz continued to influence new styles of music through the decades, from bebop, funk, rock and roll, and even hip hop.

Literature

The acclaimed American author and humorist Mark Twain wrote *The Adventures of Tom Sawyer* and *The Adventures of Huckleberry Finn*, which are today considered literary classics.

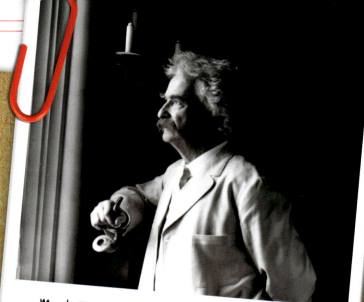
Mark Twain (Samuel L. Clemens, 1835-1910)

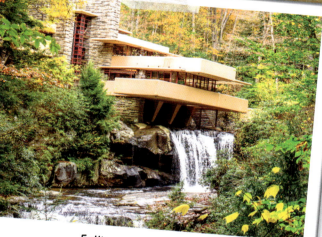
Fallingwater house
PENNSYLVANIA

Frank Lloyd Wright

Frank Lloyd Wright is one of the forerunners of Classical Modernism and he is America's most esteemed architect. Two of his works are among America's most famous, and unusual, buildings.

He designed Fallingwater in 1934 for his clients, the Kaufmann family. The interior is designed to resemble nature. The house became famous and is now a National Historic Landmark.

The Solomon R. Guggenheim Museum
NEW YORK CITY

The Solomon R. Guggenheim Museum in New York City, or the Guggenheim as it's known, is another of Wright's renowned works. The Solomon R. Guggenheim Museum opened on 21 October 1959, with 3,000 people lined up to visit.

FOOD

American food varies from region to region, but meat, poultry, fish and vegetables are widely enjoyed. Rich soil in farming regions provides abundant grains, fruits and vegetables.

Dishes incorporate influences from diverse multicultural communities, and many restaurants offer foods from all over the world. Many Americans enjoy Central and South American cuisines.

Fast Food

The US is well-known for its fast food. Over a quarter of Americans eat fast food daily because it is cheap and convenient.

ON THE MENU

Have you tried these famous North American foods?

Ribs

Americans love pork or beef ribs, slathered or smoked.

Apple Pie

Apple pie remains one of the country's most popular desserts.

Pot Roast

A favoured comfort food is the pot roast.

Buffalo Wings

Buffalo wings, despite their name, are chicken wings tossed in cayenne pepper hot sauce and butter. They were first eaten in Buffalo, New York; hence the name.

Cobb Salad

The famous Cobb salad has lettuce, watercress, tomatoes, avocado, some cold chicken breast, a hard-boiled egg, chives, cheese, and topped with French dressing.

The United States is a geographically diverse country, with stunning mountain ranges, rolling plains and valleys, river systems and lakes, and coastal areas.

There are arctic and tundra conditions in northern Alaska, while Death Valley in California is one of the hottest places on Earth. The US is the third largest country in the world. In the south, it shares a 3,111-kilometre-long border with Mexico. To the north is the 8,890-kilometre-long border with Canada.

Apart from its land borders, it is surrounded by water, with the Atlantic Ocean in the east and the Pacific Ocean in the west.

GEOGRAPHY

The Missouri River

Mighty Rivers

The longest river in the United States, and the fourth-longest river system in the world, is the Missouri River. It springs from Montana at the base of the Rocky Mountains, travelling 3,767 kilometres before emptying into the Mississippi River. The Mississippi River is another extremely important river system and home to hundreds of species of fish, birds, mammals and amphibians.

Wildfires cause devastation in California

Natural Disasters

The United States is affected by a variety of natural disasters, including floods, hurricanes, earthquakes, bushfires and tornadoes.

The Rocky Mountains

Cedar Point peninsula, Lake Erie

The Rocky Mountains

The Rocky Mountains, called 'The Rockies' for short, are a massive mountain range that run more than 4,800 kilometres through Montana, Idaho, Washington, Wyoming, Utah, Colorado and New Mexico. National parks of the region include Yellowstone, which sits on top of a dormant volcano and is home to more geysers and hot springs than any other place on Earth.

The Great Lakes

The Great Lakes are, from west to east: Superior, Michigan, Huron, Erie and Ontario. They form the largest freshwater system on Earth. The waterfalls of Niagara Falls are located on the Niagara River which connects two of the five Great Lakes, Lake Erie and Lake Ontario.

Climate

Climate varies depending on the region and geographical features. In the southern regions, the warmest temperatures are during July and August, with tropical temperatures in Florida and Hawaii. In Alaska and the Rocky Mountains, temperatures are arctic and alpine. The northeastern states experience freezing winters but can be hot in summer.

WILDLIFE

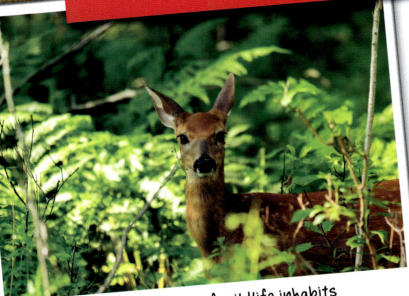

A diverse range of wildlife inhabits the USA's vast and varied landscapes

With its richly diverse geography, including mountain ranges, grasslands, and marine and freshwater regions, there are many varied habitats where species of moose, buffalo, raccoons, wild horses, wolf, cougar, coyote, deer, birds and fish can flourish. While there has been a decline in wild animal numbers, with many now on the endangered animal list, there are also many programs that work to protect the natural environment, and in turn the wildlife.

Did You Know?

The United States is one of only a few countries that have two national animals: both the bald eagle and the American bison.

American bison live mostly in large herds in Montana and in the Yellowstone National Park

The grey wolf population is again flourishing

The American beaver is found near ponds, rivers, and other slow-moving water habitats

Recognise These Animals?
Some of the United States' most recognisable animals:

The American black bear is found across the country, particularly in northeastern states

The North American cougar population is growing again, particularly in the Midwest

Bald eagles are found near rivers, lakes and along the coast

TIMELINE

'The Roaring Twenties' was also known as 'the Jazz Age'

Pre-1000 AD
Native American cultures flourish

1492
Christopher Columbus sails from Spain and lands in the Bahamas

1620
The English pilgrims arrive on the Mayflower, landing in Plymouth, Massachusetts

1789
George Washington becomes the first President of the USA

1860
Abraham Lincoln is elected President

1920 – 1929
The Roaring Twenties

1865
President Lincoln is assassinated

1000 AD
Viking Leif Erikson lands in Newfoundland, calling it Vinland

1513
Ponce de Leon of Spain lands in Florida

19 Apr 1775 – 3 Sept 1783
American War of Independence

1848
The California gold rush begins

1861 – 1865
The American Civil War between the North against the South. The North wins, leading to the end of slavery

1917
The US enters World War I

1929
The stock market crashes, leading to the Great Depression

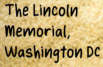

The Lincoln Memorial, Washington DC

Civil War nurses, from Harper's Weekly, 1862

The USS Arizona Memorial at Pearl Harbour, Hawaii

1941

Japan attacks the American shipping fleet at Pearl Harbour. The US enters World War II

1963

Martin Luther King Jnr delivers his speech: "I Have a Dream". The Civil Rights Act is signed by the President the following year

1968

Martin Luther King Jnr is assassinated

1955 – 1975

The Vietnam War

2003

The Iraq War begins

2017

Donald Trump becomes the 45th President and the first person without prior military or government service to hold the office

2021

20 January, Joe Biden becomes the 46th President of the United States

1963

President Kennedy is assassinated in Dallas

1945

The US drops atomic bombs on Hiroshima and Nagasaki, Japan, ending World War II

1969

Neil Armstrong becomes the first man to walk on the moon

2001

The 9/11 terrorist attacks occur

2009

Barack Obama becomes the first African American President of the United States

2020

Joe Biden defeats Donald Trump in the Presidential elections, but Trump refuses to concede defeat, claiming voter fraud and election rigging

Hiroshima Peace Memorial Park in Japan

USA 29
First Moon Landing, 1969

FLAG, SYMBOLS AND ANTHEM

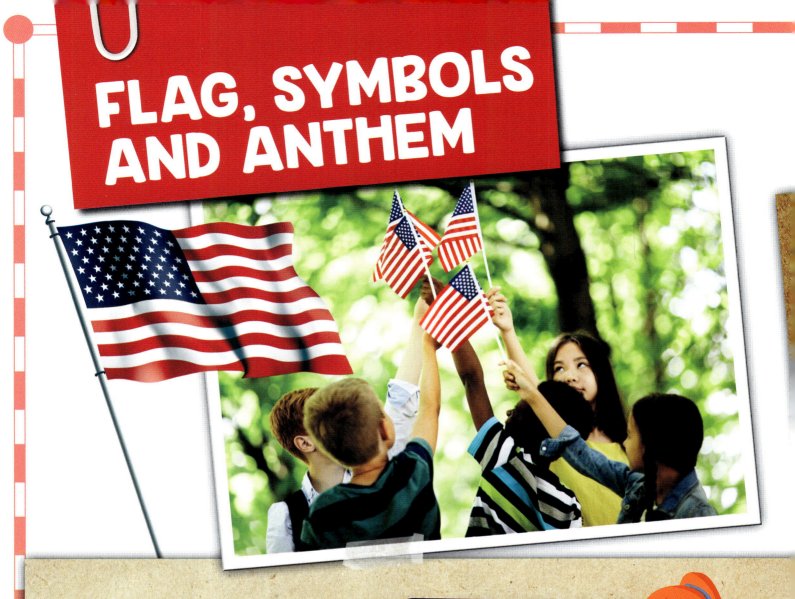

Flag of the USA

The flag of the United States is one of the most recognisable flags in the world. It has three stripes: red, white and blue. The red denotes bravery and strength, white stands for purity and innocence; and blue is for perseverance, watchfulness and justice. The flag is often called the Stars and Stripes.

National Anthem

The national anthem is *The Star Spangled Banner.*

National Bird

The national bird is the bald eagle.

National Flower

The national flower is the rose.

National Tree

The national tree is the oak.

National Animal

The national animal is the
North American bison.

GLOSSARY

Amish members of a conservative Christian Church who do not accept modern conveniences or technologies

agriculture to do with farming

American Indians the first people who lived in North America

architect person who designs a building

arid region very dry area

culture practices, beliefs and customs of a society or people

endangered when a species is at risk

ethnic referring to a group of people who share a common culture, language and heritage

export sell goods to overseas countries

film studio organisation that produces and distributes film

First Nations group of Indigenous people of the same language and cultural beliefs

gold rush rapid migration of people in search of gold

immigrant person who settles in another country

multicultural referring to a society with several different nationalities and ethnic groups

species group of living things with similar characteristics

Vikings Norse people who voyaged around Europe and North America from the 8th to the late 11th centuries

INDEX

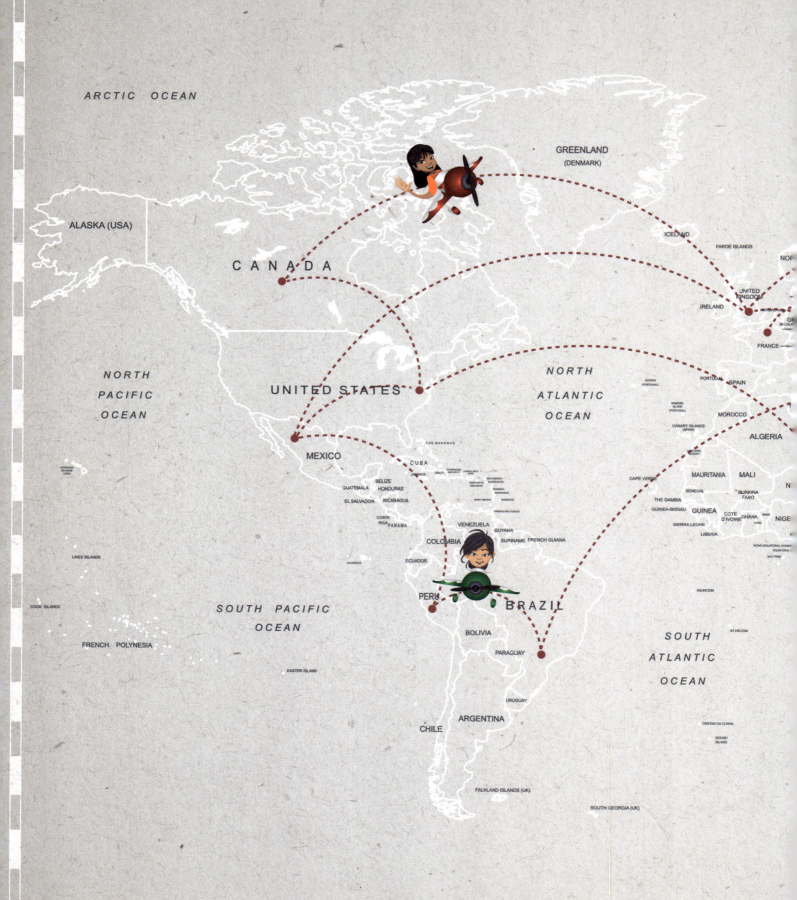